The Diamond Princess Steps Through the Mirror

THE JEWEL KINGDOM

The Diamond Princess Steps Through the Mirror

JAHNNA N. MALCOLM

Illustrations by Paul Casale

SCHOLASTIC INC.
NEW YORK   TORONTO   LONDON   AUCKLAND   SYDNEY
MEXICO CITY   NEW DELHI   HONG KONG

ISBN 0-590-97880-2

12 11 10 9 8 7 6 5 4 3 2 1   9/9 0 1 2 3 4/0

Printed in the U.S.A.   40
First Scholastic printing, May 1999

For Claude and Janine,
who will always
hold a special place in our hearts

CONTENTS

————◆————

The Diamond Princess Steps
Through the Mirror

THE JEWEL KINGDOM

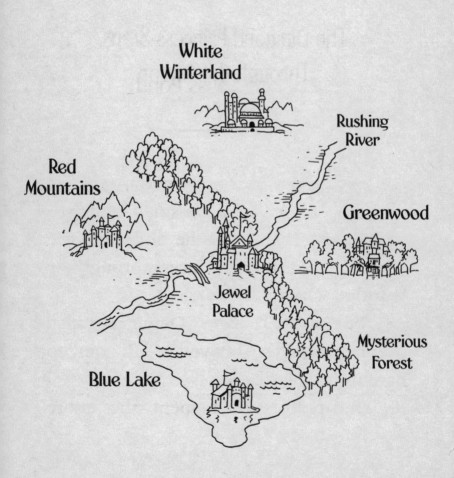

White
Winterland

Rushing
River

Red
Mountains

Greenwood

Jewel
Palace

Mysterious
Forest

Blue Lake

Looking Glass Pond

"Princess Demetra, please slow down!" a small white fox shouted as he followed the Diamond Princess through the sparkling Crystal Gardens.

"I'm sorry, Finley," Demetra called over her shoulder, "but you're just going to have to walk faster."

The princess had spent the entire

morning inside the Diamond Palace. Now she wanted to run.

"But your duties," Finley puffed as he hurried to keep up. "I have an entire page of items I need to read to you."

"Try and catch me!" Demetra said with a grin. "If you can, I'll listen to your list."

She ducked around a snowberry bush covered in icicles and raced toward Looking Glass Pond.

Finley was Demetra's palace adviser and best friend. Usually he enjoyed a good game of tag, but not today.

"Please, Princess," he begged as he raced to join her. "Let's do work first and play later."

Demetra dropped onto one of the white marble benches that surrounded the pond. Tiny snowflakes were carved into it.

"All we do is work! I want to have some fun."

"Fun?" Finley held up his paper for her to see. "This afternoon you're to greet guests from the Borderlands. You have fun with them, don't you?"

Demetra retied the bow on her thick brown braid and nodded. "Yes. I do."

"And after that, you'll be cutting the ribbon at the new snowshoe workshop. That's fun, isn't it?"

Demetra rolled her dark blue eyes. "Sometimes."

"Well, what about the sparkle flakes you're supposed to make with the Sylvan Elves from the Snowy Wood? I know you enjoy that."

Demetra sighed. "I like making sparkle flakes and seeing friends, but . . ."

Her voice trailed off. Demetra loved being a princess and didn't want to sound like she was complaining.

Finley perched on the bench next to her. "But what?"

The princess looked over both shoulders, and then whispered, "Just once, I'd like not to have my day planned for me. Sometimes I'd just like to do nothing at all."

"Oh, dear." Finley's whiskers twitched. "This is a bad day to want to do nothing. Look at this list." He tapped the paper with his paw. "And that's just for the day. Tonight you're supposed to give your harp concert."

Demetra put her chin in her hands. "What did I tell you? Every minute of today is planned."

Finley stared at the princess for a long

time. Finally he said, "Suppose someone else did a few of these duties for you. Then you'd have the afternoon off. Would that make you happy?"

"Very happy," Demetra replied. "But what someone would do that?"

Finley hopped off the bench and puffed out his chest. "Me."

Demetra's eyes widened. "Oh, Finley, do you really mean it?"

Finley nodded. "I'd do anything for you, my friend."

"A whole afternoon to do exactly what I want!" Demetra wrapped her arms around the little fox's neck. "I can't think of a nicer present!"

"So, while I'm cutting ribbons, greeting friends, and making sparkle flakes, what are you going to do?" the fox asked.

The Diamond Princess shrugged her shoulders. "I might go for a walk," she said with a smile. "Or go ice-skating right here on Looking Glass Pond."

"Well, have fun," Finley said as he turned back to the Crystal Garden. "Just be back in time for your harp concert tonight."

Demetra grinned. "I wouldn't miss it for the world."

The princess watched the white fox scurry away. Then she leaped into the air and shouted, "Hooray!"

The first thing she did was jump from one bench to another until she'd circled the pond. Then she picked a white winter pear from one of the trees and ate it.

"Mmmmmm . . ." she murmured. "Delicious."

Demetra ran to get her ice skates from

the gazebo next to the pond. She laced up her skates and stepped out onto the ice.

As she glided across Looking Glass Pond, Demetra sang to herself, "I may be a princess but I like to have fun. I may be a princess but I love to run."

The more she sang about being a princess, the more Demetra thought about her sisters.

Demetra, the eldest of the four princesses, ruled the White Winterland. Roxanne, the Ruby Princess, ruled the Red Mountains. Sabrina was the Sapphire Princess and lived in her palace at Blue Lake. Emily, the youngest, ruled the Greenwood as the Emerald Princess.

"I wonder if they ever take days off?" Demetra said out loud as she twirled around in the center of the pond. "I wonder if they'd like to be ordinary girls for once."

Demetra pulled her arms in close and spun in a tighter, faster circle. The next thing she knew, her feet slipped out from under her. Demetra fell down with a loud *thump*. Her dress spread out on the ice around her like a silvery cloud.

She wasn't hurt. She was just surprised. But there was a small tear in the hem of her gown. Demetra bent to look at it and noticed something shiny lying on the ice.

"My mirror!" she cried. The ribbon holding the mirror to her waist had snapped in the fall.

This was no ordinary mirror. It had been a gift from the great wizard Gallivant. The mirror had the power to show

Demetra what was happening in faraway places.

"I hope it's not broken," Demetra whispered as she carefully picked it up.

The mirror hadn't cracked. But something was different.

Princess Demetra looked into the mirror and gasped. She should have been looking at her own reflection, but a strange face gazed back at her. It was a girl's face.

Suddenly the girl smiled.

"Hello, I'm Lisel. Who are you?"

The Face in the Mirror

The Diamond Princess stared at the strange face in her mirror. She was so startled she couldn't speak. Finally she sputtered, "I — I'm Demetra. What are you doing in my mirror?"

"I'm not sure." The girl blinked her pale blue eyes. "I was walking across Looking Glass Pond. I raised my mirror to look into it — and there you were."

Demetra frowned. "But *I'm* standing on Looking Glass Pond and you're not here."

"Of course not, silly," the girl named Lisel answered. "I'm in Freezia."

"Freezia?" Demetra repeated. "Where's that? I live in the White Winterland."

Now it was Lisel's turn to frown. "I've never heard of the White Winterland."

"You must have," Demetra said. "It's part of the Jewel Kingdom."

Lisel shrugged. "I don't know the Jewel Kingdom."

This was very strange. Everyone knew the Jewel Kingdom. Demetra tapped her mirror.

"What are you doing?" Lisel asked.

"I'm trying to find out if you're real," Demetra said. "Maybe you're just a little bit of my mirror's magic gone wrong."

"I'm very real," Lisel huffed. "And so is Freezia. See for yourself."

The girl held the mirror so Demetra could see her land. Freezia appeared to be a land of snow and ice that looked just like Demetra's world.

"I don't understand," the princess murmured. "Where are you?"

Lisel's face reappeared in the mirror. "Maybe I'm on the other side of your looking glass."

Demetra's eyes grew into two huge blue circles. "You mean, you're in a mirror world?"

Lisel shrugged. "The Old Tales tell of a door to another world. That door could be here at Looking Glass Pond. And that would explain why one pond seems to be in two places."

"Then Looking Glass Pond must

connect our two worlds," Demetra whispered.

"Show me your world," Lisel urged.

Demetra pointed her mirror toward her crystal castle with its delicate towers. In the sunlight, it looked like a sparkling ice sculpture. "That's the Diamond Palace."

"Oooh!" Lisel gasped. "I've never seen anything so beautiful in my life. It's a castle fit for royalty."

"I *am* royalty." Demetra blushed. "I'm the Diamond Princess."

Lisel stared at Demetra in awe. "I've never met a princess before," she said. "We don't have them in Freezia."

Demetra looked closely at her new friend. Lisel was dressed all in white. Her wool jacket had a high fur collar. Little pearls were woven into the blonde braids that crossed the top of her head.

"What does a princess do, anyway?" Lisel asked. "Sit in her palace all day and order people around?"

Demetra shook her head. "It's not like that at all. There are parties I have to host, and visitors I have to greet. I travel all over my land making sure my people are happy."

"That sounds like fun," Lisel said with a sigh.

"Well, what do you do in Freezia?" Demetra asked.

A gust of wind blew snow across the mirror and then Lisel answered, "We spend most of the day with the sled."

Sledding? Demetra thought. *That sounds like fun.*

"And in the mornings we swim in the hot geyser pools."

Demetra liked swimming.

"Today," Lisel added, "I was skating across Looking Glass Pond in search of winter pears."

"Skating, swimming, sledding, eating pears," Demetra repeated. "That's what I love to do most."

Lisel blinked in surprise. "Then you would have a very good time in Freezia."

Demetra giggled. "I wish we could switch places."

Lisel wiggled her eyebrows. "Maybe we can."

"Do you think it's possible?" Demetra asked.

"Yes." Lisel leaned her face close to the mirror. "The Old Tales tell of people crossing through a magic door into another land."

"What are the Old Tales?" Demetra asked.

"The Old Tales are from a book that has been in Freezia for a very long time," Lisel replied. "It was written by the Old Ones. It is our history."

"Do the Old Tales tell you how to cross between worlds?"

Lisel squeezed her eyes shut and tried to remember. "I think you can only leave this world if someone takes your place from the other world."

Demetra shivered. What if there really was a magic door? It would be fun to pass into another world!

"We just need to find a way through," Lisel continued.

Demetra stared at the mirror glittering in her hand. "We go through my mirror," she declared. "It's magic."

"Come on," Lisel urged. "Let's try it."

Demetra was thankful that Finley was

filling in for her at the palace. She could do whatever she wanted this afternoon. Then she remembered the concert that evening. She knew she couldn't stay away for long.

"I'll do it," Demetra whispered. "But only for the day. I must come back tonight."

"Fine," Lisel said. She put her fingertips against her mirror. "Are you ready?"

"I think so." Demetra put her fingertips against her own mirror.

For a brief moment their fingers touched. Then there was a flash of light and everything went white.

Trading Places

Princess Demetra looked down at her clothes. She no longer wore her silver-and-white gown. Now she was dressed in Lisel's fur-trimmed jacket and skirt. Thick mittens covered her hands. Furry boots dressed her feet. In spite of her warm clothes, though, she still felt cold.

"Brrrr!" Demetra said between

chattering teeth. "Freezia is *much* colder than the White Winterland."

A gust of wind spun her around on the ice. Everywhere she looked Demetra saw snowy mountains and trees covered with icicles. Where were the beautiful gardens and pretty glass houses that glowed with the warm light from the crystals?

"If this is a mirror world of the White Winterland," she murmured, "it's a cracked one."

"Lisel!" A voice floated on the wind. "What are you doing?"

Demetra squinted through the snow. A woman dressed in a fur cap and a long coat trudged through the deep snow.

"Come, Lisel!" the woman shouted, cupping her mittened hands around her mouth.

"Lisel?" Demetra repeated. She looked down at her clothes. They certainly looked like Lisel's. Did that mean her face looked like Lisel's, too?

Demetra raised the mirror hanging from her waist. Her hair was still in one long braid but her face had become Lisel's face. "If the mirror's magic makes me look like Lisel," she whispered, "I'd better pretend to be Lisel." She stuck the mirror inside her coat to keep it safe.

"Hurry, dear," Lisel's mother called. "We have to get back to the sled. Karlee and Hawken are waiting for us."

"Sled?" Demetra repeated. "Where is it?"

The woman motioned for her to follow. Demetra hurried off the ice. She was looking forward to sledding.

Demetra followed Lisel's mother

around a snow-covered hill and stopped in her tracks. Ahead of her sat a giant sleigh piled high with packages. It was not the kind of sleigh she expected.

Two people ran to greet her. One was a boy who looked about her age. The girl looked a year or two younger. *They must be Hawken and Karlee*, Demetra thought.

"Lisel, did you bring the pears?" the boy asked.

Demetra winced. Lisel had said she was out picking pears. "Oops, I forgot!"

"Don't get your hopes up, Karlee." The boy turned and called to his sister. "Lisel forgot the pears. *Again.*"

Karlee wore a heavy parka, loose-fitting pants, and high boots. "Lisel!" She stomped her foot in the snow. "What were you doing, daydreaming?"

"Yes," Demetra admitted with a grin.

"I was dreaming that I talked to a princess from another world."

"What kind of world?" Hawken asked.

"One that looked like Freezia but was much warmer, with lots of beautiful homes and palaces," Demetra replied.

Karlee waved a mittened hand. "There's no such place."

"Yes, there is," Demetra said. "You just have to find the right door to go there."

Hawken threw back his head and laughed. "There you go again, believing the Old Tales." He pushed a shock of blond hair out of his blue eyes. "Papa told you not to think about them anymore."

"That's right," Karlee said, looking back at the sleigh. Their father stood talking to their mother. "They only make you sad."

"Sad?" Demetra wondered why stories

would make Lisel sad. "I don't feel sad."

Karlee nudged her brother. "Lisel *says* she's not sad, but all you have to do is talk about the warm days before the Big Freeze and her eyes will fill with tears."

Just hearing Karlee say "Big Freeze" made Demetra shiver. "I do wish it were a little warmer here," she said between chattering teeth. "Maybe we should go home now."

Hawken stared at her for a long time. "What do you mean?"

Demetra pointed to the sled piled high with packages. "Isn't it time to take the sled home?"

Karlee and Hawken looked at each other. Then Karlee whispered, "But, Lisel, the sled *is* our home."

Freezia

 Princess Demetra helped Lisel's family pull the big, heavy sled under a cliff they called Icicle Falls. She still couldn't understand why they didn't have a home with walls and a roof.

The icicles hanging over the big cliff formed a wall of ice against the wind. Demetra was glad of that.

"You children gather firewood, will

you?" Lisel's father called from the front of the sled. "Your mother and I will prepare a meal."

"Come on." Hawken tugged the sleeve of Demetra's jacket. "We'll find kindling in the woods."

Demetra followed Hawken into the grove of evergreen trees. "But everything's covered in ice," she said. "How will we ever get this to burn?"

Hawken had already scooped up an armload of wood. He stopped and stared hard at Demetra. "What's gotten into you, Lisel? If I didn't know you, I'd swear you weren't my sister."

This was the perfect opportunity for Demetra to tell him the truth, but she was afraid of what might happen.

"I have been feeling a little strange," she said as she bent to pick up a frozen

twig. "Sometimes I can't remember anything about our life before today."

"Yesterday was the same as the day before," Karlee said as she came up beside them. "We pulled the sled, hunted for firewood, skated across ice ponds looking for food — "

"And took baths in the hot springs," Demetra added, remembering Lisel's words. Not long ago, it had all sounded like fun.

"That's right," Hawken said, grinning. "It looks like your memory is coming back."

"But was there ever a time when we weren't pulling the sled?" Demetra asked.

"Of course," Karlee said. "It seems like yesterday that we were still in our home at Snowberry Meadow. And I had my own room and friends who lived next door."

Demetra put her hand to her head,

pretending to remember. "That's right," she said slowly. "But we left because . . . because it got so cold?"

"Right," Hawken said. "Everyone left Freezia to find a warmer place to live."

"But why did it suddenly turn cold?" Demetra asked. "And why didn't we just use the crystals?"

Crystal power was what kept the White Winterland warm and cozy.

"There are no more crystals. You know that," Hawken said sharply. "The crystals were a gift from the Old Ones. We weren't careful and we used them up. Freezia lost all of its heat, practically overnight."

"But there *are* more crystals," Demetra pointed to the snowy mountains. "They're all around us."

Karlee dropped her kindling and cried, "Stop it, Lisel! Stop repeating those stories.

It won't work. Papa stayed much longer than we should have because he believed the Old Tales about more crystals. Now we're the last family to leave Freezia." Karlee put her face in her hands. "I hope we find the others before we freeze to death."

Demetra blinked her eyes. "We're leaving Freezia?"

"Of course we're leaving!" Karlee stomped her foot in the snow. "Stop acting stupid. You're going to make us all crazy."

Demetra spun to face Hawken. "When? When do we leave?"

"Today. Now," he answered, never taking his eyes from her face. "This is our last stop before we cross the border."

Demetra couldn't leave. Looking Glass Pond was in Freezia. That pond was her doorway to the White Winterland.

"We can't go," the princess gasped. "If we leave I'll never be able to go home."

Demetra turned and stumbled out of the woods. She had to talk to Lisel right away. Before it was too late!

Come Back, Lisel!

 Princess Demetra ran until she found a boulder big enough to hide behind. She fumbled for the mirror at her waist.

"Please let the magic work here," she murmured as she raised the mirror in front of her.

Then Demetra chanted:

"Magic mirror, with power so bright,
Show me Lisel, use your light!"

Suddenly the mirror turned into a reflecting pool. Demetra could see Lisel, dressed in Demetra's silver-and-white gown, seated on a lovely white chair in the Great Hall of the Diamond Palace. At first it looked like she was surrounded by giggling children. Then Demetra realized the children were the Sylvan Elves.

"She's at the sparkle flakes party," Demetra murmured as she watched Lisel take a bite of frosted white cake. "That cake looks delicious."

Lisel finished the cake and then reached for another slice.

"Oh, no you don't," Demetra cried. "Save some for me!"

Lisel paused in midreach and looked over her shoulder, confused.

"Good, she can hear me," Demetra murmured. Then she cupped one hand around her mouth and shouted into the mirror. "Lisel! I'm in the mirror! Answer me!"

Lisel leaped to her feet and nearly dropped her plate. She fumbled for the mirror at her waist. Then she held it up close to her face.

"Demetra?" she whispered. "Did you call me?"

"Yes!" Demetra shouted. "We have to talk."

Lisel ducked behind one of the pillars in the Great Hall. "I don't really have time to talk," she whispered. "I'm in the middle of a party."

"That's *my* party," Demetra reminded

her. "And you're eating *my* cakes with *my* friends."

"They're wonderful creatures," Lisel said with a giggle. "We've had so much fun. We're making sparkle flakes."

Demetra rolled her eyes. "I know that. That was supposed to be me making the sparkle flakes, remember?"

Lisel didn't answer. Instead she said, "What do you want?"

"I want to come home," Demetra said firmly. "Right now."

Lisel's mouth dropped open in surprise. "But I've only started having fun."

Demetra put one hand on her hip. "Well, I haven't had any fun. You said I'd be sledding, and ice-skating — "

"And aren't you?" Lisel cut in.

"Yes, but not the kind of sledding

or skating I want to do," Demetra said. "Besides, you forgot to mention one very important thing."

"What?" Lisel asked.

"That your family is leaving Freezia," Demetra explained. "Today. This very afternoon. You know I can't go with them."

"Why not?"

"If I leave Freezia I may never be able to return to the White Winterland." Demetra swallowed hard. "We could be stuck in each other's worlds forever."

Lisel looked around at the Diamond Palace. "I wouldn't mind that at all. I like your world and your friends. And I like being warm."

"But you could be warm here," Demetra cried. "If you just found more crystals."

Demetra was about to explain how her people found crystals inside Sparkle Mountain that kept them warm, when several voices cried, "Princess!"

The Sylvan Elves were calling Lisel to join them for tea.

"Coming!" Lisel called over her shoulder. Then she whispered, "I'm sorry, but I have to go."

"Wait!" Demetra cried as a gust of cold wind blew around the boulder. "Don't leave me here! This isn't my world. It's too cold and lonely."

"I'll talk to you later," Lisel said.

Lisel slipped her mirror into the pocket of her dress and Demetra's mirror went dark.

Tell the Truth

Princess Demetra panicked. What if Lisel didn't come back? She would be stuck in this strange world forever.

"I have to tell her family the truth," Demetra cried as she ran back to join them at Icicle Falls.

When the princess arrived at the sled, Lisel's family was huddled around their campfire, eating bowls of hot stew.

"There you are," Lisel's mother said. "Karlee was afraid you'd run away. But I knew you'd be back."

Lisel's father grinned. "No one can resist your mother's delicious barley stew."

Demetra tried to return his smile. Lisel's family seemed very nice. She knew that what she was about to say would shock them. It took all of her courage to say it.

"Sit down." Lisel's mother patted the stump beside her. "Eat, before your food gets cold."

Demetra stayed standing. "I have something to tell you," she began, "but I'm not sure how to say it."

"Just tell us," Hawken said with an encouraging smile.

"All right." Demetra took a deep breath and jumped in. She told them her real name. Then she explained about taking the day off from being a princess and going ice-skating on Looking Glass Pond. Demetra explained that she had fallen and something had jolted her magic mirror.

"When I looked in the glass," she said, "there was your daughter Lisel."

Lisel's mother and father exchanged looks, but said nothing. Even Karlee was speechless. She stared at Demetra with her mouth open.

Finally Hawken said, "Go on."

Demetra explained that she and Lisel had discovered a door between two worlds. Looking Glass Pond. And that she and Lisel had decided to switch places for the day.

"But Lisel forgot to tell me you were leaving Freezia," Demetra said. "I called her with my magic mirror. But now she says she likes the White Winterland and wants to stay there."

Lisel's father blinked several times. "The White Winterland?"

"That's my home," Demetra said with a smile. "It's on the other side of the mirror. And it's almost exactly like your world. But of course it's not so cold."

"Not cold?" Lisel's mother repeated in amazement.

Demetra nodded. "That's because we use crystals mined from Sparkle Mountain. The crystals catch the sun and keep us warm. All of our homes are built with them."

"Sparkle Mountain? The Diamond Princess? A mirror world?" Lisel's father's voice grew louder with each word. "Do you expect us to believe this story?"

Demetra winced. "Yes. I do."

Lisel's father threw down his soup bowl. His face had turned a bright red. "This is it, young lady!" he shouted. "You have finally gone too far!"

Demetra turned to Karlee and Hawken. "What can I do to make you believe me?"

Karlee squinted one eye at Demetra. "If you really are a princess with magical powers, use your mirror to prove it."

Demetra looked down at the mirror at her waist. She knew she could only use the mirror three times in one day. She'd already used it twice, once to come to Freezia and once to contact Lisel. If she used it a third time, she wouldn't be able to get back to the White Winterland.

"I can't use it," she said miserably. "I have to save the magic to go home."

Karlee tossed her head. "That proves it. You are lying."

"Stop it!" Lisel's mother's voice was quiet but firm. "Karlee, I don't want to hear another word from you. Can't you see Lisel is sick?" She took off one mitten and placed her hand on Demetra's forehead. "Just as I thought. Your head is warm. You need to lie down."

"But I'm not sick," Demetra protested as they led her to the sled. "I'm telling the truth."

Lisel's mother nodded. "Of course, dear. Now, I want you to rest quietly while I make you a hot cup of honey mead tea."

As Lisel's mother hurried off to make tea, Demetra tried to think of some way to convince the family she was telling the truth before it was too late.

She lay on the sled and stared up at

Icicle Falls. They sparkled in the afternoon light.

"The crystals!" Demetra whispered. "That's it. I'll go to Sparkle Mountain myself and bring back crystals. Then they'll *have* to believe me."

Runaway Princess

 The princess waited until the family had finished eating and started cleaning their dishes. Then she slipped out of camp. In the White Winterland, Sparkle Mountain was past the Alpen Woods. Demetra knew the quickest way to get there was to take the path along Glacier's Edge, if she could just find it.

Princess Demetra followed a road that

looked like Glacier's Edge. But the road stopped at the edge of a very steep cliff.

"Where is it?" Demetra's voice echoed across the snow. "Where is Sparkle Mountain?"

The princess looked out across the valley. It was ringed by a dozen mountains. Looking Glass Pond glittered below her. But nothing else looked familiar.

"I don't know where I am," Demetra moaned as she slumped into the snow. "Now I'll never find the crystals and Lisel's family will leave Freezia."

"Demetra!" a voice called from behind her.

The princess lifted her head. All she saw was a wall of white snow. "Oh, dear," she muttered. "Now I'm starting to hear things."

Crunch. Crunch.

Footsteps! Someone was coming toward her.

"Hello?" she called. "Who's there?"

A figure clad in a fur-trimmed parka and boots suddenly appeared beside her. It was Hawken.

Demetra leaped to her feet. "W-what are you doing here?"

"I came to help you, Princess!" he replied.

"What did you say?" Demetra asked. "Did you call me 'Princess'?"

"Yes!" Hawken grinned. "I believe your story, even if the rest of my family doesn't."

Demetra shook her head. "But why?"

Hawken was pulling a toboggan with a braided rope. He slid it forward and sat down. "By the strange way you've been behaving and by your story about a place called Sparkle Mountain. The Old Tales told of more crystals. But no one ever said anything about mines inside mountains."

"I was trying to find Sparkle Mountain," Demetra explained. "There's a whole cave of crystals inside it. But I got lost."

"Maybe I can help you find it," Hawken said. "It probably has another name here in Freezia. What does it look like?"

"Like any one of those mountains." Demetra gestured to the mountain range that circled the valley. "I wish I had my map of the White Winterland. Every mountain peak is marked. It might be able to help us but it's in the palace library."

Hawken jumped to his feet. "Then let's go get the map."

"But my palace is in the White

Winterland," she said, wiping snowflakes away from her eyes. "The only way to get there is through the magic mirror at Looking Glass Pond. It's very far away and we haven't much time."

"My sled is the fastest in Freezia," Hawken declared, patting the side of the toboggan. "Hop on, Princess, and I'll take you there."

"All right," Princess Demetra said as she climbed on the sled. "But be careful."

Holding the rope in his hands, Hawken sat on the sled behind Demetra. Then he dug his heels into the snow and pushed them to the edge of the steepest cliff Demetra had ever seen.

"Hold on!" Hawken cried.

Demetra squeezed her eyes closed as the sled dipped over the edge and zoomed straight down the side of the cliff.

Just in Time

When the Diamond Princess and Hawken reached Looking Glass Pond, their cheeks and eyelashes were nearly frozen.

"You weren't kidding when you said that was a fast sled," Demetra said shakily. "One second we were on top of that cliff, and the next we were here."

"I hope you're all right," Hawken said. "I only used the brake once."

"I'm fine, thanks." Demetra rubbed her cheeks to get feeling back in them. "And I'll feel even better when we reach Lisel."

The princess stepped onto the ice. Hawken followed behind her to the center of Looking Glass Pond. Demetra clutched her mirror tightly in her hand. She knew this was the last time she could use it. She needed to talk Lisel into finding the map and returning home.

Demetra raised her mirror and chanted:

"Magic mirror, with power so bright,
Show me Lisel, use your light!"

The mirror shimmered. Soon Lisel's image came into view. She was hiding behind a purple curtain.

"Lisel!" Demetra shouted. "Look at me."

"Demetra?" Lisel whispered. "Is that you?"

"Yes!" Demetra cried. "I'm here with your brother. See?" She held the mirror so Lisel could see Hawken.

"Hawken! Demetra! You have to help me," Lisel whispered. "Everyone is looking for me and I don't know what to do."

"What's wrong?" asked Demetra.

Lisel pointed around the curtain. "A crowd is sitting in that theater waiting for me to come out and play the harp."

"But you don't play the harp," Hawken said.

"That's right." Lisel laughed shakily. "I don't play anything. I can barely sing."

Demetra put one hand to her mouth. "I forgot all about the concert. Is Finley upset?"

Lisel took another peek around the curtain. "He looks a little, um, nervous. That's because he can't find me."

"Here." Demetra reached her fingers toward the mirror. "Switch places with me and I'll play the concert."

"Wait!" Hawken grabbed Demetra's arm. "What about the crystals? You can't go until you find the map."

"Oh!" Demetra gasped. "I almost forgot." She held up the mirror and called, "Lisel, you must listen and do as I tell you."

"But the concert!" Lisel cried.

"Forget about that for now," Demetra ordered. "Go to the palace library."

"The library?" Lisel looked confused. "Why?"

"There's a map of the White Winterland hanging on the library wall.

Hawken and I need to look at that map."

Lisel peeked around the curtain again. "What if somebody sees me?" she asked in a tiny voice.

"No one will see you if you use the secret passageway," Demetra said. "See that wall behind you?"

Lisel spun around. "I see a wall but there's no door. Only a candelabra."

"Lift any one of the candles," Demetra instructed, "and that wall will become a door."

"Really?" Lisel asked in amazement.

"Yes, but hurry. It's cold out here."

Lisel was about to put away her mirror when Demetra cried, "Don't!"

"Don't what?" Lisel asked, puzzled.

"Don't leave the mirror," Demetra explained. "If we break the connection now I won't be able to reach you again until tomorrow. By then it will be too late."

Lisel did as she was told. Soon she was scurrying down a dark passage.

"The library door is at the very end," Demetra called through the mirror. "You can't miss it."

Lisel opened the door and stepped into a room filled with books.

"What a beautiful room!" Lisel gasped.

Demetra nodded wistfully. "Yes, it is."

The map of the White Winterland hung on the wall to the right of the door. Lisel stood in front of it.

"Here's the map," she said, "but why do you need it?"

"It will show us where the crystals are buried," Hawken called over Demetra's shoulder.

"Really?" Lisel gasped. "Where? Show me where they are."

"Find Looking Glass Pond," Demetra said. "Now tell me where Sparkle Mountain lies."

Lisel traced the map with one finger. "It's due west."

Demetra and Hawken turned to face west. There was no mountain there. Only the cliff they had sledded down.

"Maybe Freezia isn't a mirror world of the White Winterland, after all," Hawken said sadly.

"That's it!" Demetra cried. "It *is* a mirror world. Only it's a little cracked." She wrapped her arms around Hawken. "You're a genius."

"What?" Hawken asked, his cheeks blushing a bright red. "What did I say?"

"Everything is the exact opposite in a

mirror," Demetra explained in a rush. "So, if Sparkle Mountain lies to the west of Looking Glass Pond in the White Winterland, in Freezia — "

"It's in the east." Hawken finished her sentence. He spun and pointed to a snowcapped mountain to the east. "We call that Purple Peak in Freezia."

"Of course," Demetra said with a nod. "In a certain light, Sparkle Mountain does look purple."

"Hawken! Lisel!" an angry voice called from behind them. "It's getting late. What do you think you're doing?"

Demetra turned and gasped, "Oh, no!"

Hawken's father was marching toward the edge of Looking Glass Pond. In a matter of moments he would be at their side.

Demetra clutched Hawken's arm.

"Inside of Purple Peak is enough crystal to warm Freezia for many years to come. Tell your father."

As his father came closer and closer, Hawken whispered, "He won't believe me. What can I do?"

Demetra had to think fast. "The map!" she cried. "Lisel, pull the map off the wall and touch your mirror."

"Hurry!" Hawken cried.

As Lisel reached for the map, Hawken's father reached for Demetra's arm. "All right, young lady, you're coming with me!" he said sternly.

Demetra turned her head and said, "I'm sorry, sir, but I can't. Maybe another time."

The Diamond Princess touched her fingertips to the mirror and felt Lisel's fingertips on the other side.

"Good-bye, Hawken," Demetra cried as the glass began to wobble. "Good-bye, Lisel. Keep warm! And if you ever need me, you know where to find me."

Hawken waved. "Farewell, Princess. I'll see you in the mirror."

There was a flash of white. Suddenly, Demetra was standing in her palace library.

Before she could even catch her breath, a small white fox peeked around the library door. "There you are! We've been looking for you everywhere. The concert is about to begin."

Demetra smiled at her furry white friend. "Calm down, Finley. I'm ready. In fact, I can't wait to play for my friends."

Finley raised an eyebrow. "That's more like the Princess Demetra I know. I must say, you have been very strange all

afternoon. You acted like you were in another world."

"I *was* in a totally different world," Demetra admitted as Finley led her to the stage. When the audience saw the princess, they burst into applause. Demetra grinned at Finley and added, "And I can't tell you how glad I am to be home."

About the Authors

JAHNNA N. MALCOLM stands for Jahnna "and" Malcolm. Jahnna Beecham and Malcolm Hillgartner are married and write together. They have written over seventy books for kids. Jahnna N. Malcolm have written about ballerinas, horses, ghosts, singing cowgirls, and green slime.

Before Jahnna and Malcolm wrote books, they were actors. They met on the stage where Malcolm was playing a prince. And they were married on the stage where Jahnna was playing a princess.

Now they have their own little prince and princess: Dash and Skye. They all live in Ashland, Oregon, with their big red dog, Ruby, and their fluffy little white dog, Clarence.

Visit the authors' Web site at http://www.jewelkingdom.com.